May you have a
wonderful, Amazing Journey!
Enjoy!

Brenda Learlsen
3-22-2019

WASCANA'S AMAZING JOURNEY

Illustrated by
DOINA COCIUBA
TERRANO

BRENDA CARLSEN

Book Publishers Network
P. O. Box 2256
Bothell, WA 98041
425-483-3040
www.bookpublishersnetwork.com

Copyright 2019 © Brenda Carlsen
Illustrations by Doina Cociuba-Terrano

All rights reserved. No part of this book may be reproduced, stored in, or introduced into a retrieval system, or transmitted in any form or by any means (electronic, mechanical, photocopying, recording, or otherwise) without the prior written permission of the publisher. Printed in the U.S.A.

10 9 8 7 6 5 4 3 2 1

ISBN   978-1-948963-10-7
LCCN   2018956201

Dedication

Brenda Carlsen dedicates this book to her husband, Eric, and children, Alex, Brittany, and Ciara, who have inspired her to fly.

Doina Cociuba Terrano dedicates this book to her art, her legacy, and her children.

HONK! HONK! HONK!
The noisy gaggle of down-feathered geese flew
gracefully in the cloudy night.
FLAP . . . FLAP . . . FLAP . . . FLAP

Wascana shouted
through the wind,
"WHERE ARE WE
GOING?"
"We are flying to the
warm south for the
winter!" his friend
called back.

SWOOSH
SWOOSH
Their large silent wings pushed
the geese forward.
A few stars lit up the sky like
tiny lanterns.

2

"OUCH! OUCH!" Wascana suddenly cried.
"My wing hurts!" Wascana felt his wing
become limp.

"There is a patch of dry yellow grass below.
Let's touch down there!"
The flock of geese slowly descended.

Wascana's friend tied a sturdy green twig along his
limp wing with a stringy green piece of fern.
"Now I can fly!" Wascana jumped up.
"No," his friend replied. "Your wing is too weak.
You will fly when it is strong and powerful again."
Wascana was heartbroken. He hung his long goose
neck down over his flat webbed toes.

One goose piped up, "A few of us stay at this lake for the winter. We play in the snow till the other geese return. You can stay here too while your wing heals."
The geese all nodded in agreement.

Wascana went exploring. He cracked
the ice with his sharp beak, spread his
webbed toes, and paddled through the
frosty blue lake water. Struggling onto
the shore, his feet slipped deep into
thick grey mud, and he fell onto his
hurt wing. "OUCH! OUCH!"

Wascana tried to push himself up, but his wings and feet were covered in mucky mud. He peered through some tall, fuzzy grass and saw two GINORMOUS flat feet! Wascana tried to flap his wings and escape. He slumped onto his hurt wing. Again.

"YIKES! Your wing is injured."
Wascana let himself be scooped up by this
strange creature.
"My name is JoJo. I am going to take you to
the veterinarian. She'll fix your wing! My
hamster had a tummy ache once, and she
helped him feel better!"

The veterinarian's gentle
hands examined Wascana's
wing. "The twig and fern have
steadied this goose's wing,
but he needs to exercise to
gain strength."
"I have some super ideas!"
JoJo announced, as Wascana
nuzzled into his arms.

Wascana woke in the morning with a
bowl of fresh water and berries next to him.

"I hope you like them!" said JoJo.

Wascana scooped up the cool water with
his mouth and stretched his neck upwards
while it trickled down the back of his throat.
He pecked at the tasty blueberries until his
full belly stuck out! Startled by seeing a
reflection of himself in the kitchen window,
he let out a loud HONK!

JoJo laughed. "Hey! Your tongue is
all purple!"

JoJo led the way outside into the sparkling, sunny winter day. "It's a beautiful day to exercise that wing of yours! Let's go!"

Wascana waddled behind JoJo.

"This is a hockey stick!" JoJo held up a long wooden stick, one of his hands clutching the top of the stick and the other around the middle. He swung it back and then forward, striking a baseball-size "snowball" with the curved end of the hockey stick. The snowball flew across to the other side of the street.

"Your turn now!"
Wascana wrapped the tips of his wings along
the hockey stick, being oh-so caring of his
injured one. He struck the hard snowball
through the air, and it landed . . Right next
to him! "Try again," JoJo encouraged.

Wascana struck a hundred snowballs,
and each time they flew farther!
Sometimes he swung too fast and . . .
BAM!
He fell backwards into a snowbank
onto his big feathered bottom!

By bedtime, Wascana was SOOOO tired. He snuggled under a blanket next to JoJo.

It's cozy and warm in this soft nest, thought Wascana.

Jojo reached his hand into a big straw basket full of books. He read a book to Wascana about a pig named Wilbur and a spider named Charlotte.

He fell asleep listening to the soothing sound of Jojo's voice.

The next morning, JoJo dragged a large, strange-
looking object from underneath a pile of snow.
"Today we are going sledding."

Wascana watched JoJo grasp his fingers around the sled's
thick, rough rope. Wascana wrapped one of his wings around the
rope. They pulled the sled up the steep hill together. Wascana
dug his sharp toenails into the deep snowpack, pushing forward.

"Hop on," JoJo cried when they got to the top of the hill.

They jumped onto the red wooden sled and slid down the
crusty white snow.

Again and again, they pulled the heavy wooden sled up the
steep hill, racing to the bottom.

Sometimes they raced

so fast

and so far

and so high . . .

They flew right over treetops, over houses,
and over a crystal blue lake.
This is like flying! thought Wascana.
Goose-sized tears trickled from his eyes and
slid off the edge of his grey beak.
He remembered.

JoJo flopped backwards, plopping down on top of the snow. Feathery snowflakes landed on his cold red cheeks. He stuck out his tongue to catch them. JoJo spread his arms out from his body as he moved them up and down like wings.

Wascana gently flopped backwards too, cushioned by the soft down of his brown and white feathers. He spread his wings out and moved them

up

down

up

down

on top of the snow.

"You are making goose angels!" laughed JoJo.

Wascana opened his mouth to catch snowflakes too, tickling his thick grey tongue.

JoJo and Wascana rolled hundreds of snowballs, slid down huge hills, and made snow and goose angels all winter.

Wascana practiced flapping his wings. He flew higher in the sky.

His wings grew STRONG.

His flaps became POWERFUL.

Each cold wintery night, JoJo chose a
book from his straw basket. He read a story
to Wascana about a girl named Alice chasing
a rabbit into a deep rabbit hole.

Wascana slept peacefully listening to
JoJo's soothing voice.

Flowers began to bloom.

JoJo knew.

Wascana knew.

It's time I go.

Wascana stretched his long goose neck
towards JoJo.
FLAP . . . FLAP . . . FLAP . . . FLAP.

A
single
beautiful
brown
feather
fell.

JoJo's fingers caught the soft feather.
Wascana gave him a big GOOSE hug.

Summer ended.

JoJo gazed into the sky. Flocks of geese flapped silently through the air, flying south for the winter. He heard a familiar, HHOONNKK, HHOONNKK.

And a single brown,

soft feather

floated

down

down

down.